Ruby and Grub

Abi Burlingham
Illustrated by Sarah Warburton

little bee books

This is me.

I'm Ruby.

This is Grub.

He's a grubby, messy pup!

Grub loves to dig.
He digs and digs and digs.
When I shout,
"Stop digging!"
he doesn't stop digging.

Do you know what he does?
He keeps digging!
I don't think he can hear me.

Sometimes he turns on his side,
like this.
I say, “No, Grub, no!”
But he doesn’t listen.

I say, “Walk, Grub, walk!”
Do you know what he does?
He rolls on his other side!
I think Grub’s tired.

Sometimes, Grub rolls over and over ***so*** much that he needs a bath.

I say, "In, Grub, in!"
Do you know what he does?
He leaps in the bath,
then he rolls over and over
in the bath!

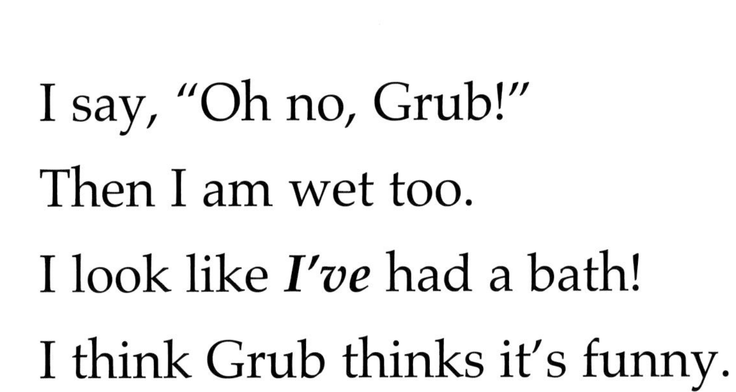

I say, "Oh no, Grub!"

Then I am wet too.

I look like ***I've*** had a bath!

I think Grub thinks it's funny.

It ***is*** quite funny.

Last week I had a tummy ache.
Grub sat by my bed
and wouldn't move–
all day!
"Bed, Grub, bed!" I said.
Do you know what he did?
He sat on ***my*** bed.
I think he thought it was ***his*** bed!

Then one day,
something ***terrible*** happened.
Grub got loose!

Do you know what he did?
He chased the ice cream truck down the street,
and the truck had to stop.

I told him, “Grub, that’s bad!”
But then I thought,
“No, it’s good,”
and I bought some ice cream.

It was delicious!
Grub thought so too.

Then one day, something even more terrible happened.
Grub dug a hole under our fence
and under our next door neighbor's fence.
It took six people to catch him and bring him back.

Mom wasn't pleased at all!
"***That is it!***" she said, "I've had enough!
Grub, you are just too naughty, too messy,
and too much trouble," she said.
"Grub, you will have to GO!"

I cried,
but Mom
wouldn't
budge.

So we took him to Uncle Tom's.
Uncle Tom had three dogs already.
He didn't mind one more.

DOG

When we got home,
it felt so strange without Grub.
I kept looking around, thinking,
"Where's Grub?"
Mom kept looking around, thinking,
"Where's Grub?"

Dad kept looking around, thinking,
"Where's Grub?"
Joe crawled around and around
the house until he was dizzy, shouting,
"***GUB! GUB!***"
The house didn't feel right
without Grub.

We stood in the garden.
It was a mess!
We filled in the holes that Grub dug.
It took ages!
Do you know what Joe did?
He started digging holes in
the garden!
It didn't feel right without Grub.

I gave Sally a bath to make me feel better.
But she didn't splash like Grub.
I splashed water on myself.
But it wasn't the same without Grub.

Mom bought us ice cream to cheer us up.
But it didn't taste the same without Grub.
Mom said, "The garden's too tidy."
Dad said, "The house is too clean."
I said, "My bed feels lonely without Grub."
Joe screwed up his face until he looked as if he'd go ***pop*** and screamed, "***GUB!!!***"

Nothing was the same without Grub.

"***That is it!***" said Mom. "I've had enough!"

"Come on, let's go," said Dad.

So Mom and Dad and Joe and I all got in the car.

Do you know where we went?

We went to Uncle Tom's!

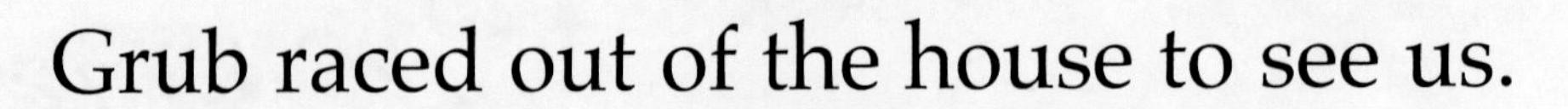

Grub raced out of the house to see us.

Do you know what he did?

He ran around in circles.

He rolled in the mud.

He covered me in muddy paw prints.

“He’s naughty, he’s messy,
and he’s far too much trouble,” said Mom.
“But we just miss him ***too*** much.”

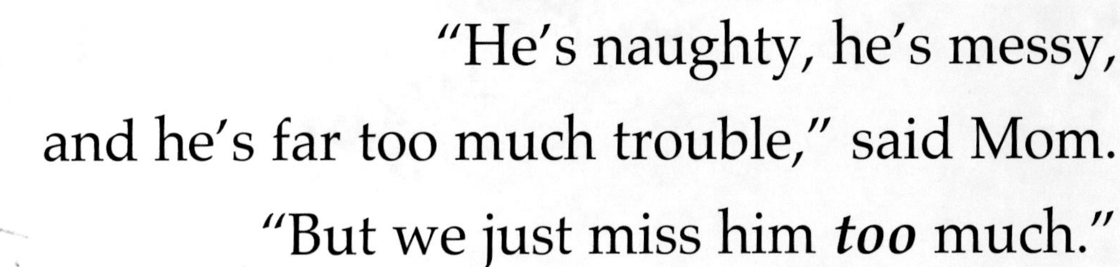

“Please can he come home?” I asked Uncle Tom.
Uncle Tom didn’t mind one bit.
He has three dogs already.

Now the house is a mess, the garden is a mess,

everywhere's a mess.

But it doesn't matter because . . .

I have Grub,

and Grub has me!